D1128432

RYE FREE READING ROOM

# Nikki Giovanni

# A Library

## Illustrated by Erin K. Robinson

VERSIFY · *An Imprint of HarperCollinsPublishers*

After breakfast on Monday,
Grandmother washes
the sheets and pillowcases.
I wash
the dishes.
I help her hang
the sheets outside
and watch the wind gently
blow them.

Grandmother takes her sit-down
and asks me:
"Aren't you going
to return those books?"

I hurry up Mulvaney Street

all the way to Vine Avenue

to the
Carnegie
Library.

A library is:

a place to be free
to be in space

to be a cook

to be a
crook

to be unhappy

Quiet Please

to be quick and smart

to be contained
and cautious

to surf
the
rainbow

to sail the dreams

to be blue

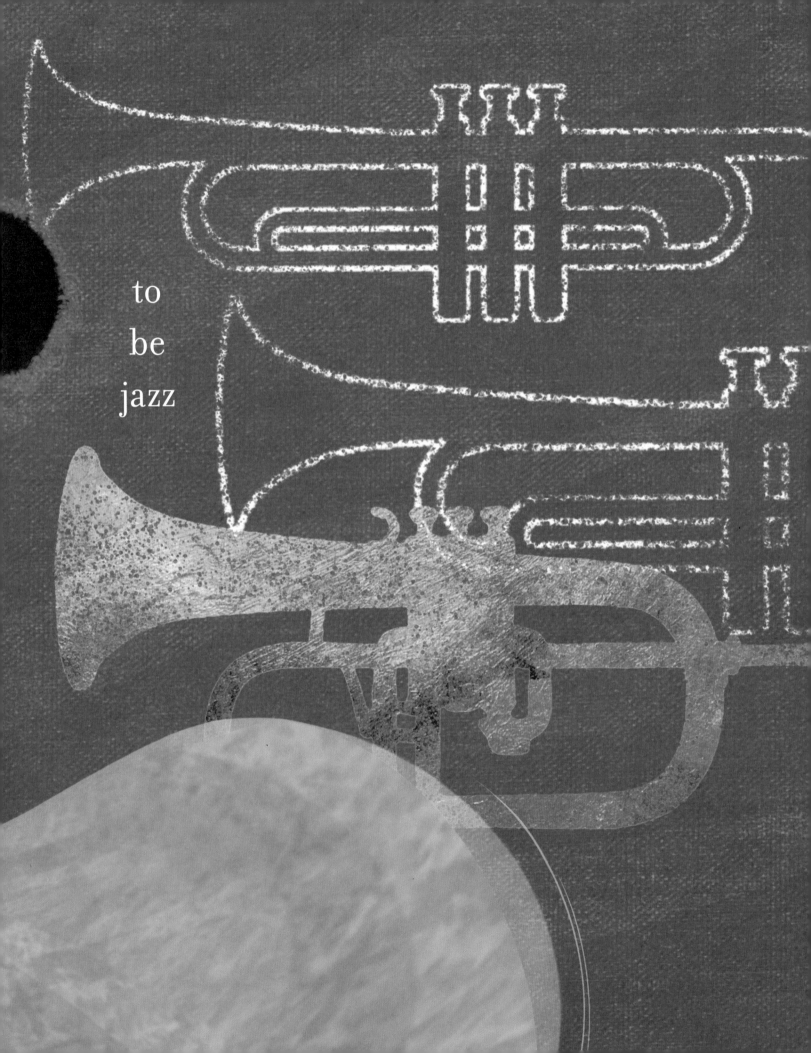

to
be
jazz

to be wonderful
to be you

a place to be
yeah . . . to be

I go home
and help fold the sheets
and peel the carrots and
potatoes and onions

and go sit on the back porch,
covering my toes with a quilt,
and read

to be
another
me.

# My Library

My first memory of my library is a big room with heavy wooden tables, heavy oak chairs, and creaky wood floors. Banker's lamps with green shades ran down the center of the tables. In the foyer, there was a semicircular desk; to the left, a card catalog; and to the right, newspapers draped over wooden dowels. There was always the welcoming smile of my librarian and the joy of so many books waiting for me.

Mrs. Long was my first librarian. I spent summers with my grandmother in Knoxville, Tennessee, and Mrs. Long was from Kansas or Iowa. She encouraged my reading and always encouraged me to go through the card catalog to see what else was there. I grew up during the age of segregation and would want to read books that were not in the Carnegie Branch of the Lawson McGhee Library, which was the colored library. Books by Walt Whitman or Alfred North Whitehead. Mrs. Long would go up to the main library to get them for me. I was almost grown before I understood what she must have gone through to get me the books I was interested in. Mrs. Long always knew what I needed.

*Nikki Giovanni*

For Kelli Martin —N.G.

To my voracious reading mother, Dianne D. Robinson —E.K.R.

Versify® is an imprint of HarperCollins Publishers.

A Library
Text copyright © 2022 by Nikki Giovanni · Illustrations copyright © 2022 by Erin K. Robinson
"A Library" from *Acolytes* by Nikki Giovanni. Copyright © 2007 by Nikki Giovanni. Used by permission of HarperCollins Publishers

All rights reserved. Manufactured in Italy.
No part of this book may be used or reproduced in any manner whatsoever without written permission
except in the case of brief quotations embodied in critical articles and reviews. For information address
HarperCollins Children's Books, a division of HarperCollins Publishers, 195 Broadway, New York, NY 10007.
www.harpercollinschildrens.com

ISBN 978-0-35-838765-7

The artist used Procreate to create the digital illustrations for this book. · Typography by Jessica Handelman

22 23 24 25 26 RTLO 10 9 8 7 6 5 4 3 2 1

First Edition

GIOVANNI
Giovanni, Nikki.
A library.
09/24/2022

GIOVANNI
Giovanni, Nikki.
A library.
09/24/2022